KAY CHORAO'S
Big Book
FOR Babies

The Baby's Good Morning Book

The Baby's Lap Book

The Baby's Bedtime Book

Barnes & Noble Books
New York

THE
Baby's
Good Morning
Book

ACKNOWLEDGMENTS

The author and publisher gratefully acknowledge permission to reprint on:

page 13, "Will There Really Be a Morning?" by Emily Dickinson, from *The Poems of Emily Dickinson,* edited by Thomas H. Johnson, published by Little, Brown and Company.

pages 18 & 19, "Ducks at Dawn" by James S. Tippett from *Crickety Cricket: The Best-Loved Poems of James S. Tippett.* Copyright 1933 by Harper & Row, Publishers, Inc. Reprinted by permission of Harper & Row, Publishers, Inc.

page 20, "Getting Out of Bed" by Eleanor Farjeon. From *Eleanor Farjeon's Poems for Children* (J. B. Lippincott Co.). Copyright 1933, 1961 by Eleanor Farjeon. Reprinted by permission of Harper & Row, Publishers, Inc. And from *Silver Sand and Snow,* published by Michael Joseph Ltd.

page 25, "Singing-Time" from *The Fairy Green* by Rose Fyleman. Copyright 1923 by George H. Doran Co. Reprinted by permission of Doubleday & Company, Inc., and The Society of Authors as the literary representative of the Estate of Rose Fyleman.

page 27, "Sunrise" from *City Sandwich* by Frank Asch. Copyright © 1978 by Frank Asch. By permission of Greenwillow Books, a Division of William Morrow & Company.

page 32, "That May Morning" from *Is Somewhere Always Far Away?* by Leland B. Jacobs. Copyright © 1967 by Leland B. Jacobs. Reprinted by permission of Holt, Rinehart and Winston, Publishers.

page 52, "Twinkletoes" from *When We Were Very Young* by A. A. Milne. Copyright 1924 by E. P. Dutton, renewed 1952 by A. A. Milne. Reprinted by permission of the publishers: E. P. Dutton, a division of New American Library, and Methuen Children's Books.

page 54, "I Am Rose" by Gertrude Stein, from *The World Is Round,* © 1966, Addison-Wesley, Reading, Massachusetts. Poem. Reprinted with permission.

Contents

Time To Rise

by Robert Louis Stevenson

A birdie with a yellow bill
Hopped upon the windowsill,
Cocked his shining eye and said:
"Ain't you 'shamed, you sleepyhead!"

Will There Really Be a Morning?

by Emily Dickinson

Will there really be a morning?
Is there such a thing as day?
Could I see it from the mountains
If I were as tall as they?

Has it feet like water-lilies?
Has it feathers like a bird?
Is it brought from famous countries
Of which I have never heard?

Oh, some scholar! Oh, some sailor!
Oh, some wise man from the skies!
Please to tell a little pilgrim
Where the place called morning lies!

A Dewdrop

Little drop of dew,
Like a gem you are;
I believe that you
Must have been a star.